Nightmare in Fairyland

a short story

Judy Lunsford

Nightmare in Fairyland

a short story

Judy Lunsford

The cemetery was rather quiet on my annual visit.

Not that the cemetery was usually a loud place, but it was otherworldly quiet.

I usually visited at night, so as to make sure that I was alone when I made my annual visit. My only company was the occasional hoot of an owl or flapping wings of a bat, the chirping of the crickets, and if it was the right time of year, the cicadas and their obnoxious chorus.

But not that particular night. It was so quiet that the silence was almost deafening.

I probably should have been scared, but then I was a person who wasn't afraid of walking through a cemetery alone at midnight under a full moon.

I could sense that something happened here. Something violent. Something magical.

People tend to be afraid of cemeteries, thinking that they are haunted. But far from it. Ghosts tend to haunt where they died, not where they were buried. Cemeteries were usually peaceful and free from ghostly hauntings.

But when I saw her, it made me wonder.

She was an older woman, probably in her 60's at least, but still rather beautiful for her age. She was dressed in overalls and a flannel shirt. I couldn't tell what color because she was a ghost, and ghosts only glowed an eerie bluish white. But she was different. She had a green aura about her that I could feel from where I stood. It was powerful, and peaceful.

She walked along the edge of the cemetery towards a large Victorian house that was on the other side of the iron fence that surrounded the cemetery.

I decided to follow her. Just because it was such a rare occurrence to see a ghost here at all.

She stood staring over the garden that was in the front yard of the house. It was a night blooming garden. There were white flowers blooming all over in the moonlight, glowing with an almost ghostly white themselves.

But then the most peculiar thing started to happen.

The most beautiful music I have ever heard started to emanate from the garden. I crept closer, not wanting to disturb the ghost as she listened to the enchanting sound.

I looked out over the garden and saw that the flowers were singing. It was a magical garden and the moon flowers wove their voices together into the most magical harmony I have ever heard.

I watched the ghost as she smiled slightly and shut her eyes so she could experience the pure enjoyment of the hypnotic melody.

I found myself shutting my eyes as well and the magic of the flowers washed over me. I could feel myself being spirited away, not completely against my will, to somewhere else.

When I opened my eyes, the cemetery and the Victorian house that loomed in the darkness on the other side of the fence were gone and I found myself somewhere else entirely.

I looked around and it was daylight. I was standing in the most magical garden I had ever seen. The colors were the most vivid and beautiful hues and I couldn't help but want to touch them.

I reached out my hand towards a bright red rose, but before I could touch it, a voice behind me stopped me.

"Don't touch it," the voice said.

I turned and saw the ghost of the old woman standing behind me.

"Where are we?" I asked.

"We're in Fairyland," she said. "You hitchhiked to a very dangerous place, at a very dangerous moment."

"And why is that?" I asked.

"I was summoned by Titania, the fairy queen, and the song that you overheard the flowers singing was the pathway to this place," she gestured around herself.

Behind her was a fountain. It had three tiers and looked so refreshing. I found myself drawn to it.

"Don't," she said, her voice in a warning tone. "Do not eat or drink anything while you are here."

"But I'm so thirsty," I said.

"No, you're not," the old woman said. "It's just an enchantment. To make you think you're thirsty. Resist it. Do whatever you have to do to resist it."

"Who are you?" I asked.

"My name is Dottie," she said. "Who are you?"

"I'm-" I started to say. But I was cut off.

"Don't," Dottie said. "Don't give anyone here your name."

"But you asked-"

"It was a test," she said. "Don't fail it again."

"You were supposed to come alone," a booming voice said.

Dottie looked around and then looked at me.

"Remember what I said," she warned. "Do not eat or drink anything while you are here. No matter how tempting. Or you will never leave."

I looked around the place and wondered why anyone would ever want to leave.

"How do I get back?" I asked.

"I'll come back for you," she said.
"Don't make any deals, and don't give a fae creature your name."

She turned away from me and approached a woman with long flowing red hair who was wearing a slinky and glittery green dress. She glared at me over Dottie's shoulder and I could hear Dottie speaking to her in a calming voice.

I decided that I wasn't welcome to hang around the private meeting between a ghost and the queen of the fairies and decided to take a closer look at the fountain.

I walked towards it, across the lush velvety green grass and stared in wonder at the vivid hues of the rainbow of color in the flowers. They seemed to grow taller as I walked along the path.

As I walked, I felt like I was being watched. I looked around and all the flowers seemed to have faces. And peeking out from behind some of them were tiny pixies that giggled as I walked past them.

As I approached the fountain, a centaur appeared from out of the forest that stood tall and mighty on the far side of the fountain.

He approached me and glared at me as I continued forward.

He was tall and majestic and carried himself with an air of confidence that I had never seen before. His muscular body was intimidating enough, but set high up on the horse's body, he towered over me. His long brown hair hung down over his shoulders and crept down his human torso along his spine.

He had a bow and a quiver of arrows, but he did not have them ready for use.

I was hoping that meant that he meant me no harm.

"What are you doing here, human?" he stared at me with piercing brown eyes.

"I am here by accident," I said. "I'm just waiting for uh my friend. I'm hoping she can help me get home."

"Make sure your time here is brief," the centaur said. "We don't like having your kind meddling in our business."

The centaur snorted at me with disgust and walked back towards the trees.

"Don't mind him," a little voice said to me. "The centaurs are just big bullies."

I looked towards the voice and saw a small blue pixie looking at me with her wide eyes. Her blue hair was so long that it covered her completely and she hovered beside me with a light blue dust trailing from her all the way down to the ground.

"He didn't seem like he meant any harm," I shrugged.

"Not now he didn't," the pixie said. "But later, you just wait, you'll see him again."

There was a bubbling sound coming from the fountain, I turned to look and a green horse-like creature with a long tail like a fish emerged from the water. It had fangs and was dripping with a mane of seaweed.

"What the-" I backed away from the creature.

I looked around for the blue pixie, but she had completely disappeared.

"Come here," a voice said.

I looked next to the creature and saw what looked like a mermaid sitting on the edge of the fountain.

I shook my head, as I looked back at the horse-creature.

"Come here," she said again. "My kelpie has bad eyesight, and she would like to get a better look at you."

"No," I said. "That's okay, I'd best be getting back to my friend."

I tried to turn away, but the mermaid had started to sing. Her song was making my feet move like they had a mind of their own, drawing me nearer and nearer to her.

"Put your hands over your ears," something whispered to me.

I clapped my hands over my ears so hard I almost made my own knees buckle from the sound. But it helped to block the mermaid's voice.

"Run," the whisper said. "Run while you still have the strength."

I turned and ran as hard and as fast as I could. I could hear the mermaid calling out to me, but her singing had stopped.

"Please, come back," she cried. "My kelpie is so hungry."

I didn't turn to look behind me, and apparently, I wasn't paying attention to where I was going, so I wound up in the woods somehow.

I didn't even think I had been running in that direction, but suddenly, it was as if the forest had just sprung up around me.

The pine trees were so tall that they seemed to block out the sun. Daylight had disappeared completely and when I looked up, I could see a smattering of stars in the dark night sky above me.

It was dark, but there were tiny little lights that lit up in the air around me.

At first, I thought they were fireflies, but upon closer examination, they were pixies with tiny little lanterns that they held up in front of them.

"Follow us," they said. "We will lead you to safety."

The lantern pixies lined up and created a path through the forest.

I should have listened to my gut and not followed them, but I was to the point that I just wanted to get out of the darkness. I didn't know what was creeping around out there, so I had no idea what was hiding and waiting to kill me or eat me in the dark recesses of the woods.

The little fairy lights led me to a small hut in the middle of the forest. There was smoke rising from the chimney and the windows revealed light coming from the inside.

"There, there," the pixies whispered. "Go in there, she will keep you safe."

I walked up the stone pathway that led to the door and I knocked.

The door was made out of planks of wood and looked rickety and unstable.

I heard footsteps from inside and then the door opened.

I was greeted by the smell of something that smelled absolutely wonderful that was cooking over the fire in the fireplace, and an old woman, hunched over from age, stood in the doorway.

"Can I help you?" she asked.

"I got lost in the forest," I said. "The pixies led me here. They told me you could keep me safe."

"Oh, certainly," she held the door open wide. "Come in, come in."

I entered the small hut and was greeted by warmth and the wonderful smell coming from a pot that dangled over the fire.

The place was cozy, with a bed in one corner, a table with two chairs near the fire, and shelves that filled the walls around the rest of the small single room hut.

There were books and miscellaneous items that filled the shelves. Small bottles, jars, and decanters of various sizes were interspersed among the books, and a skeleton sat on the shelf nearest the fire. It was small, but not humanoid in shape.

"I see you've noticed Igor," she said, nodding to the skull. "He likes it over where it is warm."

"Who was Igor?" I asked.

"He is my familiar," she said. "A wonderful cat. He ran out of lives, but he still continues on, as loyal as ever."

I looked back over at the skeletal creature and it lifted its head as if looking at me. Its empty eyes stared at me and then the head lowered back down, as if it had no interest in me whatsoever.

"Would you like some dinner?' the old woman asked. "You must be hungry."

She pulled her dark shawl tighter around her shoulders and walked over to the pot to give it a stir.

"No, thank you. I was warned not to eat or drink anything while I am here," I said. "But I appreciate the offer."

The old woman smiled at me.

She seemed like she was getting older by the minute.

She had started out looking like she was in her 60's or 70's, but now it was as if she was melting and becoming older. Her skin was wrinkling more and her hair started to fall out in clumps.

"What is happening to you?" I asked.

"Oh, darn," she said, putting her hand to her head. "My illusion spells usually last a little longer."

"I uh," I started to back away towards the door.

Things were getting too weird for me.

I started to stumble backwards, because the floor felt like it was shaking underneath me.

"What is that?" I asked.

"Oh, they're coming back," she said. "I can't seem to get rid of those pesky trolls."

"Trolls?" I scrambled to my feet.

"Yes," the old woman said. "They've been bothering me for weeks. Help me to get rid of them and I will help you find your way out of the forest."

I remembered what I was told about not making deals, so I hesitated.

Before I could say anything in response, the roof of the hut was torn off and a large green face was staring down at us.

"I told you to get out of my forest, hag," the troll said, with a voice so loud and so deep that it shook the trees.

"It's my forest," the hag said. "I was here first."

"It belongs to us now," the troll said.

I backed out the front door and stumbled onto the stone walkway.

There were three trolls that surrounded the hag's hut, and they were all looking down at her as she argued with them.

I decided it was best to slip away quietly and leave her to her debate.

I didn't see what I could do to help her, and I didn't want to accidentally stumble into a deal by helping her to battle something that I clearly could be of no help with.

I staggered to my feet and dashed off into the forest as the hag started to battle with the trolls.

I ran through the forest in the darkness, tripping over roots and small rocks and plants as I went. I struggled to get my bearings and figure out which way I had come.

The ghost and the fairy queen had to be finished with whatever conversation they were planning on having, and I needed to find Dottie. She was the only way I knew how to get home.

I struggled my way through the forest and slammed right into something solid and furry in the darkness.

I fell backwards and landed sprawled in the moss and undergrowth, looking up at the silhouette of the creature in front of me.

It turned around and I could see that it was rather large and had huge, coiled horns on the sides of his head.

He held up a lantern to look at me and I could see the hairy face of a minotaur staring down at me.

I struggled to my feet and tried to run, but the creature reached out and grabbed me by the collar of my shirt and held me up in front of his face to get a better look at me.

His teeth were long and sharp and protruded out of his mouth in an evil smile as he nodded and set me back down on the ground.

He let out an evil laugh and said, "And so the hunt begins. Run!"

He didn't have to tell me twice. I turned and ran through the forest and tried to dodge trees as I went. It was so dark; I couldn't see what direction I was running in. I just ran. I didn't like the look of the minotaur and I really didn't want him to catch me.

I could hear him laughing behind me as he started to count to ten.

My head start, I assumed.

As I ran, the mushrooms on the ground started to glow, illuminating the forest floor so I could see where to run without tripping on the roots and rocks that littered the forest floor.

I followed them until I came upon a winged horse.

A pegasus.

I hoped that this was a creature that I could trust.

I could hear the minotaur closing in behind me and I decided that the pegasus was more trustworthy than the creature chasing me.

I ran up to her and she lowered herself down so that I could climb up onto her back.

I scrambled up onto her and she took off into the air, just before the minotaur reached us.

"No fair," the minotaur yelled after me. "You cheated."

"Thank you," I said to the pegasus as we soared through the air.

"Foolish human," she said as she flew. "Your ghost friend sent me to find you."

"You know Dottie?" I asked.

"I will take you to her," the pegasus said. "But you must promise to never return."

"She told me not to make any deals," I said hesitantly.

I looked down at the earth far below me and hoped that the horse wouldn't just buck me off and leave me to fall to my death.

"No deal," the pegasus said. "Just don't come back."

"I had no plans to come here in the first place," I said.

I picked my words carefully as we conversed.

"Down here," the pegasus said as we touched down in the center of the garden, a safe distance from the fountain.

The mermaid and the kelpie were gone, but I didn't trust them to be gone for long.

Dottie stood waiting for me and looked at me impatiently.

"Where did you go?" she asked me.

"Thank you," I whispered to the pegasus as I slid off of her back.

She whinnied at me and took off into the air.

"I didn't mean to wander off," I said. "It just sort of happened."

"Did you follow the rules?" she asked me.

"I think so," I said. "Can we go home now?"

Dottie nodded and started to walk away.

"Follow me," she said. "And listen to the music. Listen for the same melody that brought you here."

I strained my ears to listen for the melodious voices of the flowers that brought me here. I stayed focused on the ghost in front of me and followed her until we were standing in front of the iron fence that separated the cemetery from the garden that resided in the front yard of the Victorian house.

The crickets chirped all around us and I was welcomed by the light of the full moon.

"Don't ever follow me again," Dottie said.

"I didn't mean to follow you the first time," I said.

She looked at me closely and then she smiled widely.

"You're here for a reason," she said.

"I was here to visit my grandmother," I said. I gestured back at the graveyard.

"She used to live in this house," Dottie gestured to the old Victorian that was on the other side of the fence.

I nodded. "Someone else owns it now."

"I know the girl who lives there now," Dottie said. "She is a very powerful mage. You must go and learn from her."

"Learn from her?" I asked. "What, just knock on the door and ask her to teach me magic or something?"

"Your power is very strong," Dottie nodded. "That is why you could follow me into Fairyland so easily. You must learn to use your powers in order to protect yourself for doing anything else just as stupid as you did tonight."

"I don't believe in magic," I said.

"Oh really?' Dottie laughed. "Then what is it that happened here tonight?"

"It was a nightmare, right?" I said. "That's the only explanation."

"No," Dottie shook her head. "You're a mage. That's how you got into Fairyland. That's why the hag didn't eat you, that's why the minotaur wanted to hunt you, and that is the only reason why you were able to mount and ride a pegasi."

"I'm not a mage," I said. "I don't even know what that means."

"If you don't know what it means to be a mage, how do you know you aren't one?" Dottie asked.

"I just-" I stared at her. "I just know."

"Yes, because it is totally normal for an average person to be standing in a cemetery at midnight having an argument with a ghost about what happened earlier in the evening while in Fairyland," Dottie said.

I heard a door shut behind me and I turned to see a goth girl of about 25 coming towards us through the glowing white flower garden. Her short black hair was cut into a bob and her black eyeliner looked like she had just rubbed her eyes from waking up. She was wearing a black t-shirt with a black miniskirt and was barefoot as she walked through the garden.

"Dottie?" the girl called out. "Who are you talking to?"

"Your new apprentice," Dottie said.

"Uh, no I'm not-" I started. I turned to the girl. "I'm not a mage."

The girl came over to the fence and looked through the iron at me.

"Not yet," the girl winked at me. "I've been waiting here all evening. What took you so long?"

More books by Judy Lunsford:

The Bird Lady: 10th Anniversary Special Edition
Seeds of Today

The Portal Wars
The Grimoires

Gamers
Schemers

Fire Lily
Bezbell
Kirog

Moonlight Magic
Moonlight Melody

The Red Dart
Shadow Mountain
Crafting Christmas

For YA:
Life Unscripted
The Secret Gondal Society

Short Story Collections:
Dark of Night, The
Fae Reign
Fairy Short Stories
Fairy Tales & Nightmares
Fantasy Faire
First Stories
Magic from the Dark
Story Hoard
The Wild Hunt

Thank you for reading.
If you enjoyed this book, you can find more stories
at
JudyLunsford.com
or your favorite online retailer.

Some gardens grow a lot more than just magic.
Moonlight Magic
Judy Lunsford

www.ingramcontent.com/pod-product-compliance
Lightning Source LLC
Chambersburg PA
CBHW070006180726
48002CB00019B/2576